Happy Eas

1977

Love from
Grammie
and
Boompa

From his home on the other side of the moon, Father Time summoned eight of his most trusted storytellers to bring a message of hope to all children. Their mission was to spread magical tales throughout the world: tales that remind us that we all belong to one family, one world; that our hearts speak the same language, no matter where we live or how different we look or sound; and that we each have the right to be loved, to be nurtured, and to reach for a dream.

This is one of their stories.
Listen with your heart and share the magic.

FOR SYLVIE AND
HER UNCLE RICK,
WHOSE CAPACITY
TO LOVE HAS
AWAKENED OUR
HEARTS.

Our thanks to artists Shanna Grotenhuis, Jane Portaluppi, and Mindi Sarko,
as well as Sharon Beckett, Yoshie Brady, Andrea Cascardi, Solveig Chandler, Jun Deguchi,
Akiko Eguchi, Liz Gordon, Tetsuo Ishida, William Levy, Michael Lynton, Masaru Nakamura,
Steve Ouimet, Tomoko Sato, Isamu Senda, Minoru Shibuya, Jan Smith, and Hideaki Suda.

THE STAR GIFT

Inspired by a Grimm Fairy Tale

Flavia Weedn & Lisa Weedn Gilbert

Illustrated by Flavia Weedn

Hyperion • New York

Once upon a time there lived a little girl who was all alone in the world and very poor. She had nowhere to live. All she had were the clothes she wore, a scarf, and one piece of bread.

She thought that if she walked through the forest, she might find a town on the other side. There, she hoped, she would meet someone who could help her find food and clothing, and a place to sleep in exchange for work.

So the little girl set out on a journey.

She had not gone far into the forest when she came upon a beggar. "Little girl," he said, "I am very hungry. Please give me your piece of bread so that I do not starve."

The girl was very hungry, too, but because she was so kind and unselfish, she gave the man her piece of bread and kept on walking.

She walked for a very long time and began
to grow tired, but she could not stop to rest
because she was still in the forest and she
knew it would soon be dark.

She met a woman who came to her and said, "Little girl, my head is so cold from the wind; please give me your scarf to help keep me warm."

The little girl's head was cold from the wind, too, but because she was so kind and unselfish, she gave the woman her scarf and went on her way.

It was getting dark now, but the little girl kept on walking, in hopes of finding shelter for the night.

Soon she came upon another child, a little boy.

He was shivering from the cold and said to the little girl, "I am very cold, and your jacket would keep me warm. Please, may I have it?" And although the little girl knew she might freeze without her jacket, she gave it to the little boy and continued on her journey.

By now it had grown very dark and very cold, and
the little girl was deep into the forest when she met
yet another child.

This child sat huddled against a tree, almost frozen from the cold. And when the poor little girl saw her, she said, "Here, I will give you my dress. It will help protect you from the cold."

She knew that if she gave her dress away, she would have only her apron to wear, but because she was so kind and unselfish, she gave her dress to the child and went on her way.

Seeing a glow in the distance, the little girl thought she had almost reached the town she had hoped for. But when she climbed up on a tree limb for a closer look, she saw it was only the moon shining down into the forest.

The poor little girl, too cold and weak to go any farther, sat down under the tree, wrapped the apron around her, and tried to cover herself with leaves. She was colder and weaker than she had ever been before.

Then the little girl began to cry because she was so frightened and alone. Through her tears she looked up into the sky and wondered what would happen to her. Seeing the beautiful stars, she made a quiet wish and then fell asleep.

Suddenly the little girl was awakened when a star from the heavens fell from the sky . . . and then another and another.

The brilliant stars were falling down to earth all around her, and she quickly stood up, watching them in wonder.

The little girl began to catch the stars in her apron, until it overflowed with sparkling brilliance. And then, quite magically, the stars began to cast a bright light before her and embraced her with a cloak of warmth.

As the stars continued to fall, they created a pathway through the forest, and the little girl began to hear the faint sound of music in the distance. The stars moved forward, as if to guide her, and she followed their warmth and light.

As she walked, the music
grew louder and louder, and
soon there appeared before
her a small house, with smoke
rising from the chimney. She
saw a family gathered on the
porch playing music.

She walked toward the house, and just as
suddenly as the stars had appeared, they vanished.
Now, except for the light coming from the house,
the forest again was dark.

Before she could say a word, the music stopped. As she looked at the family, she heard a tender voice say, "Hello, little girl! Where have you come from? You look all alone and so cold and hungry. We'd like to welcome you to our home. Please, come inside and we shall feed you and keep you warm."

The little girl could hardly believe it because this is exactly what she had wished for.

She entered the house,
and soon the little girl was
wrapped in a blanket, sitting
next to a warm fire, eating
muffins and drinking cider.
The family played beautiful
music for her, and she shared
with them her story of how
she had followed the starlight
and how it had led her to
their home.

She had no way of knowing that this family, too, had made a wish that night. They had wished for another child to join their family, a little girl just like her. Although they had not seen the path of light, nor twinkling stars, they knew this special little girl had been led to them for a reason . . . and that their wish was also coming true tonight. And because she was gentle, kind, and unselfish, the family loved her so much that they asked her to stay and live with them forever. With joy, the little girl agreed.

It was a most magical night for everyone, and happiness filled their home, but silently each of them wondered . . . Had the stars been watching this little girl from the night sky all along her journey? Had they witnessed her kind and giving nature, and had they really come down to Earth to help guide her way? Or had she simply dreamed it all?

The answer came later that night, as the family tucked the little girl into a warm bed. They wrapped a blanket around her, and the little girl felt something in her apron pocket. When she reached inside, a light filled the room, and out fell a hundred twinkling stars. Once again music filled the air, but this time it came from the sky above.

And then, with love in their hearts, they
all thanked the heavens for what they had
learned that day . . . that giving what you
have brings love in return . . . and that
somehow, someway, heaven always hears
our every wish.

Produced in cooperation with Dream Maker Studios AG.
Printed in Singapore.
For information address Hyperion Books for Children,
114 Fifth Avenue, New York, New York 10011.

FIRST EDITION
1 3 5 7 9 10 8 6 4 2

Library of Congress Cataloging-in-Publication Data

Weedn, Flavia
The star gift: inspired by a Grimm fairy tale/Flavia Weedn & Lisa Weedn Gilbert;
illustrated by Flavia Weedn—1st ed.
p. cm.—(Flavia dream maker stories)
Summary: A poor but kind and unselfish young girl who is all alone
in the world is led by the stars to a loving family.
ISBN 0-7868-0122-0
[1. Folklore—Germany.] I. Gilbert, Lisa Weedn. II. Title.
III. Series: Weedn, Flavia. Flavia dream maker stories.
PZ8.1.W43St   1995
[E] 398.2 '0943—dc20   94-36989

The artwork for each picture is digitally mastered using acrylic on canvas.
This book is set in 17-point Bernhard Modern.